The
Willow
Elf

P. S. Ellis

Matador
Unit E2 Airfield Business Park,
Harrison Road, Market Harborough,
Leicestershire. LE16 7UL
Tel: 0116 2792299
Email: books@troubador.co.uk
Web: www.troubador.co.uk/matador
Twitter: @matadorbooks

ISBN 978 1800465 190

British Library Cataloguing in Publication Data.
A catalogue record for this book is available from the British Library.

Typeset in 11pt Minion Pro by Troubador Publishing Ltd, Leicester, UK

Matador is an imprint of Troubador Publishing Ltd

For Sophie Star

Contents

1

The Spiral Earth Tone

1414, English/Welsh border

The willow tree elf sat alone. He had lived on his own for a long time amongst the many varieties of willow trees, but something today made him feel lonely. He narrowed his eyes and sniffed the air. As he thought, little gongs chimed and sang in the air.

Never before had he seen so much... space. He squeezed his eyes closed and scratched his hairy chin. His head grumbled to him that something was not right. As he thought to himself, little gongs sounded mysteriously in the air. Reluctantly, he opened his eyes. Never before had his world appeared so… bright.

This is unusual and unsettling, thought the willow elf. He liked to live in half-light and in the shadows.

He prowled the earth at night, and he was never out walking during the day. Moreover, he noticed a sour smell in the air that tickled his nostrils.

He listened to the trees, but they were unusually silent. His ears rotated forwards and backwards. Forwards and backwards. In fact, his ears turned so far back that the tips touched each other and gave him quite a fright. He did not know what to do. He wondered if he should be asking questions, but there was no one here to ask.

Why is there so much light?

As he thought, the sound of tiny gongs jangled in the woodland.

The air sparkles and shines, but with what mystery?

He looked closer and realised the air was full of flies and dust shining in, in… *daylight.* He was not used to being in daylight because he was a nocturnal creature. However, he knew daylight made flowers open and birds sing. The willow elf wondered why he was not safely tucked-up and asleep in his usual tree. The air filled with the sound of little gongs bonging as the elf thought.

Looking at his toes, the willow elf saw a fluffy yellow ochre substance lying on the ground. *It must have fallen from the sky*, thought the willow elf, but that did not feel right. If he were going to be honest with himself, he would eventually have to admit that nothing felt right today. Nothing felt normal. He struggled to see clearly in the daylight. The willow elf doodled squiggles with his toes in the dusty stuff until the sun set on the horizon.

All of a sudden, he felt himself pulled backwards as if invisible hands pulled him away. He knew what was going to happen next. The elf Ancients were calling the elves to a meeting. At any moment, he would travel backwards to an otherworldly dimension and find himself floating in a secret meeting place known as the Spiral Earth Tone where the elf Ancients held their meetings. As his feet left the ground and he rose shakily up into the air, his stomach did its usual heave.

Whoosh…

Off he flew like a dry old leaf on a stormy day. The long hairs protruding from around his ears pointed forwards and tickled his nose. It was a familiar, dizzy feeling of falling, ever so awkwardly, backwards and then upwards into a spiral. He wished that sometimes there could be a little hint as to when the elf Ancients decided to hold a meeting, but he always forgot to ask them about it, and he was sure that they would not entertain his request. He knew that the elf Ancients were all very old and that they only called the elves together when something important had happened.

When the willow elf stopped moving backwards, he spiralled upwards. He liked this part. It was like sitting on a soft, comfortable chair swinging and rotating in a greater spiral. As he moved upwards, he regained some control and looked around. It pleased him that he did not seem to be the only one who found the experience disorientating. When he saw other elves trying to find their balance, he smiled an elfish smile. Some of the elves held their big noses slightly in the air as if this would help them balance. Others tweaked their ears as they stilled themselves. Some elves continued to wobble around with their hands and feet splayed out like lizards. The willow elf could see quite a number of different tree elves. Today, there were not just willow elves but hazel tree elves, poplar tree elves, beech tree elves and ash tree elves.

"We summoned this meeting because of a disturbance in the woods that we cannot understand."

All the elves heard the voice, which sounded in the air like a deep gong. There could be no mistaking that this was a serious problem. None of the willow elves knew what had happened. The willow elf could not explain why he had been out in the daylight, nor could he explain the increased amount of space. Elves were not prone to guesswork, or superstitious suggestions, so they all kept quiet. The voice boomed again.

"Walk! Use your song and find answers."

As the willow elf spun out of the Spiral Earth Tone and back to his wood, he wondered how old the elf Ancients were and how old one had to be, to be called *Ancient*. He knew that they were so old that they no longer spoke to each other. When they needed to speak, they thought together. Tonight, they had thought and spoken as one. The willow elf decided that they must be very old indeed.

Once he was back in his patch of moonlit woodland, the willow elf picked up a handful of fluffy, yellow stuff. He sniffed it. It smelt familiar, but for some reason it made him feel terribly sad. The willow elf pulled himself up straight. He decided that he was going to be the one who went on a land voyage to seek the answers. After all, the elf Ancients had told the willow elves to *walk*, and this was going to be the adventure of his lifetime. With a spring in his bandy legs and a flick of his big feet, he started walking. He was going to search every nook and cranny of every forest, even if that meant taking a walk on the wild side.

2

The Little People

The willow elf did not get far before he decided to
investigate the yellow, fluffy stuff on the ground.
He wondered what would happen if he blew on it. As he
thought this, a small breeze lifted some of the fluffy stuff into
the air. He jumped up onto a big rock to get a better look.
The fluffy stuff danced around for a while and then floated
slowly back down to the ground. The willow elf sat down on
one of the many rough yellow discs that littered the floor. He
wondered why he had never before seen the gold-coloured

discs or the creamy, yellow stuff. It was too big to be pollen and too hard to be petals. *It smells woody*, he thought to himself. If only he could get help from someone to answer his questions. The sound of gongs bathed the moonlit air.

At that moment, something loud whizzed past his ear. He turned quickly, but he did not see anything unusual. It happened again, but this time the sound was faster and of a higher pitch.

Pizzz…

And then,

Whizzzzzzz…

The willow elf was sure that faeries flew around and whizzed about.

"We are not—" came a voice.

"Faeries!" a second one finished what the first one had started saying.

"Yes, you are," said the the willow elf watching for little people with wings dart through the air.

"No," began one of the little people.

"We're not," continued another.

The willow elf puzzled over their words. What else could they be? As he thought hard about what they had said, his eyes moved in towards the centre of his head and focused on the end of his nose. Tiny gongs jangled in the air, and he frowned. At the same time, he could hear a variety of whizzing and pizzing noises all round his head.

"You are making a lot of bonging and gonging noises," said someone.

"I can't help it. When an elf thinks, their thoughts float outside of their head, and it sounds like little gongs echoing in and out of time."

"And you look funny when you concentrate," someone chuckled.

"Is that what concentrating does to you?" asked something else.

The willow elf swung his arm around in the air to make the buzzing things go away.

"Hey!" said something in protest.

"Right then, time for introductions. I'm called Whiz. This is Whuz. That is Puzz and Pizz."

"You're all faeries," declared the willow elf, looking at four little people with wings.

As he jumped off the rock to move away from them, one of the little people yanked his ear so hard that it felt as though a pin were driven into it.

"That hurt," complained the willow elf as he gathered his limbs back together. He stood up, then rubbed his ear and belly at the same time.

"You're not listening," said someone.

"Well, what are you then?" the willow elf asked.

"Sprites," said Whuz.

"Will-o'-the-wisps," said Pizz.

"Glamours," said Puzz.

"Orbs," said Whiz.

"*Anything* but faeries," two of them said at the same time.

The willow elf was quite confused, but he had not had such a long conversation for some time, and he began to feel interested.

"What's a faery, then?"

They were quiet for a while before they answered him. When they spoke, their voices were hushed.

"You wouldn't know one if you met one," whispered Pizz.

The willow elf grunted.

"They are so bright—" began Whuz.

"Yes! So bright that you couldn't look straight at them," said Puzz.

That must be awful, thought the willow elf. He did not like too much brightness.

"And so *big*," finished Whiz, spreading his arms wide.

As the willow elf thought for a while, tiny gongs chorused in the air.

The little people listened to the familiar gongs as the willow elf thought. Then, they began to feel bored, so one of them spoke.

"Do you want to know what all this yellow, fluffy stuff is at your feet?"

The willow elf stared at his feet and nodded his head.

"Friend…" began Puzz.

"We don't bring good news," said Pizz.

The willow elf picked up the yellow stuff and smelt it. It had such a nice stinky smell.

"Like a faery, you've never seen it before," said Whuz.

Whiz continued, "And therefore you don't know what, what—"

"What you are looking at," finished Whuz.

The willow elf had a terrible sinking feeling, as though he had stepped into a huge muddy puddle and could not get out.

"It is dust from the saw," said someone quietly.

"It's wood," said someone softly. "Tree shavings."

"Sawdust."

"I'm afraid they've cut down your willow trees," whispered Pizz.

"Who has cut down all my trees? Why?"

The willow elf wondered so hard that his eyes began to cross over, and then he fell down onto the ground and wept.

"You've never lived without the trees," said Whuz.

"And therefore, you can't imagine a life without them," whispered Whiz.

The willow elf looked through teary eyes, and he wondered why these little sprites had never spoken to him before. Everything looked blurred, but it was true – he could not see his beloved trees. He wanted to ask the sprites why he had not realised the trees were gone.

"Who cut down my willow trees?" asked the willow elf.

"The men did," said someone quietly.

"They seemed interested in the branches, but once they had them, they cut down the trunks for firewood," said someone else.

The sprites watched as the willow elf rubbed his face in the soil and blew his nose on a muddy hand. They stopped hovering and sat side by side on a tree stump like a row of baby wrens. They knew that willow elves only rubbed their faces in the soil when they were very, very unhappy.

3

Walking

The willow elf had been sitting on the ground for a long time. His face was dirty with dry mud and snot. Ever since the elf Ancients had instructed their elves to *walk* and *sing*, he had been daydreaming and feeling miserable because the sprites had given him the dreadful news.

He had lost his home. Never before had he been without his trees. For hundreds of years, elves had climbed them, hidden in them, sung to them, hugged them and been very happy elves. He stood up, stumbled around for a moment and then wandered over to the river that swirled past his patch of the landscape, where he dropped down on the bank.

The willow elf sat on the edge of the river and looked at the willow leaves trapped on the surface of the water by twigs and stones. He wished that the leaves could float away instead of not knowing which way to turn, like him, so he jumped in and splashed about, cleaning the bank. There, he found some feathers, some yew berries that a bird had spat out and some elder leaves. He jumped back up onto the bank and foraged in the twigs and stones, where he found little purple and yellow flowers in the grass. When he came across a huddle of delicate tiny mushrooms, he wondered if the sprites visited these fungi.

He wondered if he could magic the willow trees back to life. There were some little willow trees growing here and there, but they would take time to mature. The willow elf wanted his big willows back now; he did not want to wait. Usually, willow elves could dream things into the here and now, but no matter how much he wished for the big trees to return, he could not do the magic. The wood shavings would not stick back together.

Four sprites were watching silently on a tree stump. Each one of them was holding on to the other's tongue so that they could not talk. They had decided amongst themselves that it was indeed a mystery that the willow elf had not noticed the missing trees. The sprites were sure that something uncanny was at work in the woods. They were waiting for the willow elf to get up and walk. All four of the little people felt responsible for the elf because they had told him the truth. They could not leave him until he found his song and started to walk.

The willow elf rubbed his nose on the back of his hand and sniffed. He decided the only thing worth doing was walking because this was what made him happy. It was his favourite type of work, and after all, it was an elf's main purpose. Feeling a little happier, the elf started to remember things. He remembered that the earth listens to elf songs and she is soothed by their singing. Then, he remembered that human beings have this ability too, but they rarely sing their songs to the earth, only to each other. Usually, it was only a person of magical lineage who eventually became aware of this wonderful co-creative opportunity. He wondered if he needed to find a magical person to help him. He jumped up and started to walk. The little people let go of each other's tongues and sighed with relief.

"Where's he off to?" said Puzz, wiping dribble from her mouth.

"I'm worried about him. Do you think he'll be alright on his own?" said Pizz.

They fluttered around like four confused butterflies until he was out of sight.

Maybe walking will make things better, thought the willow elf to himself. At least he would not be thinking. As he walked, he looked at his feet. *Plod. Plod. Thump. Plod.* The willow elf never felt weary when he was walking. He had big feet, which were flat and bouncy, and he was very good at jumping over bushes and springing over streams.

"With one eye on the weather and our toes on the tide, we'll both go together and set these songbirds free." He sang an old, merry tune and felt much better.

It started to rain. He ploughed on, with his head raised to the sky, feeling every delightful splash on his face, and collected raindrops in his mouth. The rain made him feel good. After a while, he felt quite dizzy from bending backwards to catch drops of rain, so he straightened up and looked about him. On the leaves, the rain was gathering in globules that reflected the light from the sky. *They look like white balls of magic*, thought the willow elf to himself. Everything looked so beautiful, apart from the odd-looking chap standing over there by a group of elder bushes.

The willow elf had spied another elf who was leaning lazily against a tree trunk. The other elf wore a russet-coloured waistcoat. He had heard the willow elf walking through the long, wet grass with his big, heavy feet. When he saw the willow elf staring at him, he jumped and blew an enormous raspberry in the willow elf's direction. The willow elf decided the elves in this place must be a bit strange, and he stared back at the other elf. The elf in the waistcoat seemed shocked that the willow elf could see him. *Elves don't wear clothes*, thought the willow elf. He turned and walked off in the opposite direction. Soon, he heard footsteps whipping through the grass. He turned to see the silly elf behind him.

The elf in the waistcoat stuck his leg out and pointed at his big toe.

"Where art thou off to, wise elf?" he said as he bowed before the willow elf, waved his soft pointy hat and winked.

The willow elf wondered in what century the elf belonged. Maybe he was from the future. Stranger still, was the fact that he was being funny. Deliberately. The willow elf bowed back to the strange fellow.

"I'm walking to sing and singing to walk," he said rather proudly.

"Then, I shalt *join you*, oh, Great Walking Elf, in a *merry caper!*" and the elf in the waistcoat put on his hat and leaped about in a most peculiar fashion.

"I am fine on my own, thank you," said the willow elf, preferring to be on his own. He headed off in the direction of the hills and resumed his song.

Choosing to ignore his comment, the clothed elf twirled and jumped along behind him. The willow elf heard bells ringing. The strange elf had bells tied round his ankles, a large bell on the top of his hat and sewn into the rim of the hat, were red elder berries. The willow elf asked him if he was an elder tree elf and the elf pirouetted in the air.

"How wise thou art, elf. I supply the jokes to King Henry the Fifth's court jesters. Moreover, I will have you know, it is a wonderful vocation. So, do not even think about mocking me, for I shall mock thee first."

"How do you do that?"

"Mock?"

"No! Supply jokes," said the willow elf.

The elder elf drew close and put his mouth by the willow elf's huge ear.

"I whisper into their ears and they think that they have thought of the jokes, but it was *moi* all along."

The willow elf smiled at the elder tree elf. He knew that elder elves were the wisest of all the elves and usually the most private, but he had never crossed paths with one before. He wondered if the solitude made them all a little nutty. Little gongs chimed in the air.

"Thinking? Dreaming again, art thou, Willow Elf?" said the elder tree elf.

The willow elf nodded. It was one thing he did well.

Dream. He often found answers by daydreaming.

The elder elf paused, held out his hat again, as if waiting for a golden coin, and announced in a theatrical manner, "Willow elves do not stop to ponder the world of humans, but they do such things as dream."

The willow elf decided that this elf was indeed crazy.

"Oh! Don't be *glum*, my companion, for *aye* have cometh to cheereth, you upeth!"

All elves had their own unique qualities, marvelled the willow elf: the willow elves could magic things into being by dreaming about them; elder tree elves could be wise when it was least expected; holly elves understood pain in a way that no one else did, and because of this, they were full of love. Hawthorn elves... he did not want to think too much about them, for they were the consorts to dragons.

4

The Genius Loci

After all the time he had spent with the elder elf, he had not yet reached the hills. The elder elf had danced off at sunrise when the willow elf had slept during the day, and he had not returned at sunset.

"Stop thinking so much," said a whizzing noise in his ear.

The willow elf spun around, but he could not see anyone.

"You make such a racket when you think. All that gonging and jingling and jangling never did anyone any good," said Pizz in his other ear.

"It'll all be fine, you know," said Puzz thoughtfully.

The air sounded with a sad gong.

"Do you know your nose looks like it melted in the sun?"

"Ssshhhh!" hissed Whiz.

"How did you find me?" asked the willow elf.

"See that bush over yonder?" asked Whiz.

The willow elf looked ahead. He could see many hawthorn bushes, and he nodded.

"That's *our* bush," said Whuz.

The willow elf closed his eyes to concentrate. He could not think or see clearly with all the chattering around his head.

"If I make too much noise when I think, I'll sing instead!" The willow elf started to sing. "I am singing to myself. I am singing for myself. I hold my arms up in hope of answers…"

He stomped away from the sprites and headed towards the hills and waterfalls, where he knew he would be able to dream his magic more easily. He bounced onwards with his big feet and sang. A racket of gongs jingled, as the moon rose higher in the sky.

Up in the hills, heather and bracken spilled over the earth in purple and yellow blankets. The willow elf followed a narrow sheep path as he made his way further into the valley. Up here, the air, water and earth were full of magical creatures. In fact, there were so many that the willow elf did not take much notice of the otherworldly creatures who heard his song. An adder slithered across the path ahead and a sheep bleated when an imp was sitting in the patch of grass that he wanted to chomp.

The willow elf had been trying to dream up the answers that the elf Ancients sought. He had been walking for some time. But, after all the walking in the hills and all the singing he had done over the last few days, he found himself back home. His nose must have led him back to the tree stumps where the grand willow trees had once towered over him. He could not believe he had walked in a circle.

All of a sudden, he heard a loud sigh. It was like the sighs the willow used to make in the wind, but now that they were all gone, it could not be a tree. Then, he remembered that he had seen an ancient and wide willow, which had not been cut down because it was too big to be useful. He sprang over to it. It was quiet. He made himself become still like a stone. He began to wonder if this was a trick.

Then, the willow elf heard moaning. He listened in and hoped that standing still would make him invisible. Then, he heard weeping. *Someone must be very sad*, he thought, and he felt brave.

"Where are you? I can't see you anywhere!" he said.

"That's because I am everywhere," something moaned.

The willow elf's eyes crossed over as he tried to work out what the thing had just said.

"I am the spirit of this place," said something.

The willow elf could not understand why he had not seen this creature before.

"What do you look like then?"

"I look like this place!" said the thing, sounding a little bored.

"I don't understand."

"I am the Genius Loci. The *spirit* of this *place*," the thing said.

"Why are you crying?"

"Can't you see that I am badly wounded?"

Suddenly, it made sense; the Genius Loci was weeping because he had lost his willow trees; he had lost his arms, legs and his body. He wanted his trees back as much as the willow elf did. The willow elf felt terribly sad, and he lay down to rub his face in the soil.

"On your feet, Great Elf. You are not a little creature who gives up and crumbles. You are wise, and I need your help. Bring me back my limbs and my life!"

"But I have tried," called out the willow elf.

"Use your magic. Do something. Anything," the Genius Loci sobbed.

5

The Scunner

The willow elf sat alone and shivered. He knew it was not in an elf's nature to ask for help, but clearly, this was a time to ask somebody for help, and that someone, or something, could not be an elf. There was still much confusion amongst the elves as to why the trees were cut down. The willow elf shuddered at the thought of whom he should see. He knew the elves would advise against it. As he rubbed his arms at the thought of the creature, he heard a faint whizzing or pizzing noise in the distance. He scelfed before the sprites could change his mind, which meant that he used his magic to instantly disappear from his clearing and reappear in a green valley in Wales.

The Scunner made herself difficult to find. Today, she hid under a stone. When she felt like it, she could make herself huge, and when she had enough of everything or anything, she could make herself shrink. Tonight, she was tiny and tired. Tomorrow, she would be angry and gigantic. The next day… well, she was not sure yet. She would decide later. She liked the world dark, and she liked the world damp. It suited her needs, and it suited her craft. Tonight, however, she sensed that something was searching for her and so she squeezed herself until she shrunk into a grey slug.

Once the willow elf had scelfed into a small valley laid with grass, he took a moment to look around. Underneath his feet, there was a carpet of thick spongy moss and lichen. Little blue lights shimmered in rock pools as water sprites played in the moonlight. The willow elf slipped on a slimy, smooth stone but jumped clear of the water. He knew that the Scunner would be nearby. He did not know how he knew. He just knew. He closed his eyes and dreamt about how much he wanted her help. Nothing happened. He crunched his eyes closed again, wiggled his ears and thought harder.

A clatter of gongs sounded in the valley.

The elf thought of all the yellow dust, the space and the light, which disturbed him so much, and he tried to magic the Scunner close to him. Still, nothing happened. As he began to daydream about his willow trees and how lovely they looked in summer, the Scunner squelched out from under her rock.

The willow elf watched the thing taking shape near the stones. It seemed unsure of what form to take. At first, he thought she was going to be a kind of fishy thing with too many arms and legs, and then she became all hairy, until she finally settled on the form of a woman.

The Scunner had heard such a clatter of gongs in the air and she was not pleased. Before she realised that the elf was watching her, she glowered at the world. When her eyes focused in on the willow elf, she tilted her head to one side and tried to muster a sweet smile. What a racket the willow elf made when he wanted something.

"I need to repair my home. The woods. I want to put back the willow trees," said the elf.

"I'll need something from you first, *Willow* Elf, but then, you already know that!"

The elf was dreading this bit. As long as she did not want a strand of hair, he would be fine.

"A hair from your ear," she announced with glee.

Elves' hairs did not come out easily. He closed his mouth tightly shut, and he did not move.

"And your name, elf?"

"*No!*"

"You came for my help." She turned away from him, washed her hands and feet in a nearby stream, then found a boulder to sit on, where she arranged little twigs on the top of her head.

The willow elf thought for a while and, reluctantly, he started to yank at a hair. It would not budge. He tried again. Elf hairs do not come out easily. She knew that. His head rumbled, and he felt angry. His hair would not come out. There was only one thing to do: to ask her for help.

The Scunner leaped to her feet. She carefully inspected his hairs and selected a particularly long one. She put both hands on the hair, lodged one foot firmly on the ground, one on the elf's face, and pulled. After some time had passed, the hair gave up and squelched out. The Scunner fell over backwards but held up the hair in both hands. The elf was not happy. His eyes watered. The pore that had contained the hair hurt and stuck out from his face like a volcanic crater.

The Scunner wandered off with her new and treasured possession.

"My name—" began the elf.

"Oh, I *know* your name now. Silly elf," said the Scunner, waving the hair at him. She sat down again on a mossy stone and played with the strand of hair. She stretched it. She smelled it. She listened to it. She tasted it, and then she ate it.

The willow elf wished she had not eaten it for it made him feel sick. After the sun and moon had been and gone twice, the willow elf asked the Scunner if she had his answer.

The Scunner patted her hair, which was now full of leaves.

"You cannot put the trees back. You cannot have things the way you had them before man interfered with the woods."

The willow elf could not believe it. He had waited all this time only for his question to be rubbished, and he had given her a strand of hair and his name.

"You can't simply put them back, and I cannot help you. Only man, or nature, can put them back," she laughed at him. "I wondered how long you were going to wait, stupid elf."

The elf steadied himself, held his head high and looked deep into the Scunner's eyes, for he was her equal and she ought to remember that. She had the power of sight, but he was an elf.

When she realised that her eyes were locked on to the elf's as though some invisible glue held them in place, she squirmed uncomfortably and started to shift into something with feathers. The elf remained focused and swiftly cast a spell. The Scunner came back into the shape of a woman. She was unable to shapeshift. Realising the elf had locked her into one form, she screamed out in anger but found herself alone.

The elf had scelfed.

6

The Human Den

A man called Owain jumped over a drystone dyke and stumbled over the bumpy earth. In his hand, he held a large basket and on his shoulder was a spade. He made his way to a stream and started to dig five small holes along its bank, all of which were five strides apart. Unknown to Owain either, the willow elf was sitting on a lumpy tree root that had burst out of the ground.

The willow elf had not spotted Owain, for he was watching a herd of deer on the other side of the stream, who were resting in a meadow with long grass. He watched the fawns on their wobbly legs, and it made him think about how willow branches could bend and bounce back. Birds sang to each other in the nearby trees, and ducks flew overhead. The willow elf stood up, left his seat at the edge of the forest and wandered into the long grass to stand amongst the deer.

The stags sensed him, had a good look at him and turned away. The hinds sniffed him, and since they could smell no fear or any threat from the inquisitive willow elf, they left him to wander around their herd. Suddenly, the air rippled with a queer sound, and something shot through the air, narrowly missing a hind. The willow elf threw himself down into the grass, and when he raised his head, he saw an arrow sticking into the ground like a cruel plant. He knew that men used these wooden spears, which they propelled through the air, but he did not like them.

The deer leaped around in shock and jumped over him as they fled towards the safety of trees. The willow elf watched the deer dart across the landscape and wished them safe passage into the forest. As the rumble of their hoofs left him, he suddenly felt a *smack* on the back of his head. He fell face down in the grass but bounced back up. A fawn was running as fast as he could on his willowy legs to catch up with the herd. He did not manage to run in a straight line but eventually caught up with his mother at the edge of the forest.

Hisssss!

Another arrow hurtled through the air and landed at the perimeter of the forest. The willow elf rubbed the back of his head where the young deer had clonked him with his hoof. The remainder of the herd disappeared further into the trees. Using long strides, he hurried to find the deer. Once he had caught up with them, he spied the little one with wobbly legs and decided to spend a little time with him. The willow elf kept the fawn company for a while. After having an eyebrow or two raised at him by other does, he heard a man whistling to himself. The willow elf moved his large sound receptors around and realised that the sound was coming from the outskirts of the forest. He plodded off to investigate.

Far away on the horizon, the willow elf saw a band of men with bows and arrows. As the willow elf walked away from them, he heard the man closer by whistling again. No matter how many times the willow elf tried, his mouth would not whistle. He pursed his lips together, hoping for the sound to come out.

The willow elf found the source of the whistling. Along the side of a gentle river was a man, digging holes and pushing small plants into the ground with his fingers. The willow elf wondered what type of vegetable the man was planting and he moved closer to get a better look. On the grass was a huge wicker basket. The willow elf frowned at the sight of the woven willow branches, but he knew this man was not the man who had cut down the trees, for his whistling was too cheery and his attention to plants was too kind. The willow elf peered into the basket. To his surprise, he saw many willow saplings, which were neatly arranged in bundles. The elf was confused. He had never heard of a man who planted trees.

Taking a good look at the man's face, the willow elf scelfed back in time.

The man's cottage was at the edge of a forest, which was thick with oak, holly and hazel. There, he saw the man collecting willow catkins and planting them into tiny clay pots. When no one was looking, the man whistled to the catkins, watered them and tended the soil. Excited by this new development, the willow elf scelfed backwards and forwards in time, until one day, when the young trees were stronger, the man found a spot near water and planted them. *This is the most wonderful and bizarre human being*, thought the elf. Then, the willow elf heard a woman calling to the man.

She was calling, "Owain! Oooowainnnn!"

At the sound of her voice, the man stopped his whistling and his gardening. He concealed his basket under a holly bush and headed off in her direction to a little house.

The willow elf followed him to a cottage with smoke rising out of a chimneystack. Owain removed his boots and went inside, whereupon the willow elf snuck in behind him as he closed the door. A baby was sitting propped up on a bed of woollens and sheepskins. He gazed around the room with a heavy and wobbly head. The elf crept into the cottage. He had never been inside a human den before, and he was unsure as to how this was going to work. He knew that elves could visit human dwellings because humans could not see them, but if there were rules, they were unknown to him. He moved as slowly as an elf could and stalked across the floor.

Just as he reached the centre of the room, the baby yelled an earth-shattering scream. The willow elf got such a shock that his skin wobbled like soft rubber. He jumped high into the air and froze, motionless, in the centre of the room. Slowly, he moved his eyes to look at the baby. It was staring at him. The elf scelfed to behind a wooden dresser.

Rushing over to the baby, the mother scooped him up in her arms and started chatting in the baby's language.

"*Babi!* Mama's baba. Babi! Doo-doo. Awh! Babi," she crooned.

The baby calmed, enjoyed a cuddle and then she placed him back on his soft, safe place of blankets, where he resumed his looking around.

The willow elf had never heard of a human baby who could see elves. *It's not in any elf lore*, he thought. He braved himself and stepped out from behind the dresser.

This time, the baby whipped his head round and waved a little hand.

"Aaaaaahh, aaaaa, aaaaa," it said, and when no one paid him any attention, it screamed again.

The elf shot to the other side of the room and remained hidden for some time. He wondered how the baby could see him. Reluctantly, he decided to hide until the whole household had gone to sleep. He could wait and watch for days if he needed, but he must find out why Owain was growing willow trees. He sat hidden on a shelf near some large clay storage jars. It became dark and the family fell asleep. An owl hooted outside. He was answered by another owl in the distance and then another, even further away. Listening from behind the clay pots, the willow elf waited. Just as he crept out from his hiding space, a small elf scelfed into the house and appeared at the side of the human's bed.

The willow elf jumped back behind the pots. The little elf crawled onto the sheepskins on the bed and sat next to the man's head. The willow elf watched, unmoving from his shelf. The little elf rubbed his toes, picked his teeth and then made himself comfortable. Then, a sweet-sounding song reached the willow elf's inner ear. The little elf was weaving the air with his fingers and singing, ever so quietly, into the man's ear. This continued for some time until the baby woke up and started to cry. The little elf did not scelf but hid by the side of the bed. The mother sat by the ash of the fire and fed her baby. She rubbed his back. Once the baby was sleeping, she put him into his crib, and they fell asleep.

The little elf began to sing again. When the night was fully dark and the moon was high but hidden amongst clouds, the little elf pulled out a small willow wand. The willow elf held his breath. The little elf carefully pushed the wand underneath the layers of wool and sheepskin where the man slept. The man began to see dreams that he had never dreamt before. They were vivid, playful and full of activity.

The willow elf was shocked. This was unheard of and it was not allowed. He rotated his ears forwards and tuned in to the little elf's giggle of gongs. This lasted for most of the night. When the owls began to grumble about the night becoming day, the little elf clumsily stood, stretched his arms up into the air, smiled and, in an instant, he scelfed. The baby woke up, started crying for milk and the willow elf scelfed back to his tree stumps.

Back in his clearing, the willow elf understood what had happened in the human's den. Although the little elf had been naughty, he had also been resourceful and cunning. The little elf had been instructing and encouraging the man to plant young willow trees. The willow elf would stay close to the human today and do whatever he could to help the man tend to his young willow trees.

7

The Red Elf

Owain washed the soil from his hands in a stream that ran by his cottage, and as he did this, he looked over his shoulder. The willow elf began to realise that the longer he hung around this human being, the more the man looked about him, as though he were looking for someone. He would dig and pack soil for a while, look over his shoulder again, scratch his head and turn around to continue. He patted the soil around the young willows and gently pushed them down into the earth.

"There's someone watching me. I know there is," said Owain when he came home to his cottage.

"Rubbish! You're losing the plot, man," said his wife Jessie. Owain stood in the doorway and stared out into the gloomy evening light. "Anyway, what are you doing, wasting your time planting trees? No one in their right mind plants *trees*," she said, as she fed their baby.

"But I can make willow baskets and sell them at market. Also, willow makes good bows and arrows. The bark and leaves can be made into a remedy to cure aches and pains," he replied.

"Really?"

"Toothache, headaches, women's problems and fevers," he said proudly.

"I knew I'd married a clever man," Jessie said.

Owain was clearly feeling uncomfortable as the elf watched him because, as he spoke, he kept looking up to where the willow elf sat in a tree. The willow elf decided that he did not want Owain to feel worried, and he scelfed to a different part of the land.

In his new location, the wind was low. The deer and rabbits relished the mild breeze on their fur. Stomping through brambles, the willow elf was thinking about his willow trees' branches swaying in autumn. Quite unexpectedly, the willow elf found himself walking in a dark part of the forest that was new to him. He slowed his pace and looked around. There was much mud where men had walked and, feeling curious, he followed the bumpy track left by horses and carts. He jumped over the puddles that had formed in the gullies, leaped over squelchy pools and practised balancing on the raised parts of earth.

Ahead, he could see more discs like the ones in his patch of the forest, but these were a red colour. Cautiously, he approached the clearing and placed his hand on a tree stump. He sensed that these were altogether different types of trees and that their magical properties were much heavier, and more serious, than those of willow. Out of the corner of his eye, he saw a red ball of light. It looked out of place, for it did not roll on the ground, but it darted side to side in the air. He turned and stared at it. The red ball of light was undecided about which way to go.

The willow elf began to believe that something odd was afoot. He stepped back. He wondered why men had chopped down so many of these trees, for it was not a seasonal activity of collecting firewood; people usually collected deadwood for their fires. Gongs jangled in the warm air as he wondered what was so special about these trees. The red orb became brighter and the willow elf wished that he did not make so much noise when he thought. Suddenly, the willow elf jumped as the orb of light burst, and standing next to him was a red elf shaking a staff and wiggling his fingers and toes.

The red elf glowered and the willow elf thought that he really ought to stop thinking. Maybe his thoughts disturbed this elf. Gradually, the sound of gongs quietened, until the only noises were that of mice, squirrels and birds foraging in the forest. Blinking, the red elf looked at the willow elf. His expression relaxed a little, but he still looked rather grumpy. Gongs rumbled in the air again. The willow elf held his breath.

Stop thinking, thought the willow elf.

The red elf scowled and stared at him. They continued like this for a few minutes, with the willow elf wondering when the best time would be to leave. Eventually, the willow elf plucked up the courage to say goodbye and bowed his head politely. In exchange, the red elf bowed his head and as he did so, the willow elf immediately knew what troubled the other elf. This elf was a yew tree elf and the King's men had chopped down many yew trees to carve into fighting tools. In his mind flashed images of huge bows the same height as the men.

The willow elf stumbled over the mud. His situation was suddenly an awkward one. How would he communicate this delicate and bad news to the yew tree elf? Hopefully, the red elf already knew his thoughts. The willow elf remembered that yew trees were the trees of death because they gave passage across the threshold of this world into the afterlife for magical beings and humans.

The sound of gongs precipitated in the air like rain that was threatening to pour down. The willow elf wondered if the red elf could carry him away into the afterlife before he was ready. He did not know yew tree magic. He liked being here in the wet, muddy forest. He did not want the yew elf to get any dark thoughts in his head because, although the willow elf was troubled too, he was out and about seeking answers. Deciding it was time to be brave, the willow elf asked the yew elf if he could be on his way, and he apologised for disturbing him.

The yew tree elf held up his staff and the willow elf halted mid-stride. A deep roaring noise, like that of Owain's fire rushing up his chimney, grabbed the willow elf's attention. He tried to remember if he had ever come across a yew elf. He remembered being nearby one a few times, but there had been no need for conversation. Although the willow elf was very old, he had lived a private life. There were many creatures in the natural atmosphere, but most magical creatures passed each other with silent acknowledgement. He thought to himself that mutual appreciation and peace is how nature and magic worked best.

The rumbling sound quietened. The willow elf put a hand on his tummy. Nope. It was not his belly that rumbled. Then, he placed a hand on his head. Yes, the sound was in his head. It was the yew tree elf communicating with him.

"Why do humans not pay attention to what grows here? Every tree grows with patience where seeds fall. Many seeds are here. Destruction is not the true path of magic but the route of man."

The willow elf nodded in agreement. He told him he was determined to find out what was going on and that he would try to fix it. He told him of his willow trees and together their expressions darkened.

"Why were you in a ball of light?" asked the willow elf.

"I've been like that since the men came. I've been hiding like that so long, I thought I'd got stuck. I tried to hide but you'd seen me. That's how they see us, you know, as little lights. When we come across them humans, we yew tree elves jump up out of the earth and trees and become walkers of air. When they see little orbs of light, they think they're just imagining things."

The willow elf thought that he could try that for fun one day, but he told the other elf that he was on an important walk and that he would come back to see him when he knew more.

As he turned to leave, the red elf spoke. "It stunks."

"What stunks?"

"The air stunks!"

"Ah! The air stinks. That's the, the… that'll be the…"

The willow elf remembered the sour smell of the willow shavings. He could not tell him the smell was from yew tree shavings. He did not want the red elf to get more upset or angry. The sound of little gongs banged in the woods as the willow elf thought. The red elf looked around him. The willow elf politely said goodbye and scelfed.

8

The Faery

In a forest far away, a gong chimed quietly in the air. It made a lonesome noise. The willow elf wondered how he had not known the forest was in danger. Why did men need the willow trees? Why did none of the elves see or hear the trees being cut down? He wondered what he could do.

The willow elf tried to stop thinking, just in case anyone heard him. Nevertheless, the willow elf sorely missed the willow trees and the swishing of the branches. He missed their squeaking and squealing sounds when the wind pulled at their limbs. He missed the twist and turn of the fibres in the winter weather. He missed sitting inside the trunks listening to the rise of their sap in spring. Willow trees sighed together so beautifully, remembered the elf. He missed swinging on the branches that dangled over the river and jumping to the other side of the bank. There must have been many woodcutters, but for some reason they had left one enormous willow tree in the clearing. The willow elf wondered if they had decided that this tree was useless because it was too difficult to chop up, too old, or too wise...

In an instant, he had scelfed back to his tree stumps and leaped up onto the ancient willow's branches. The tree made him feel so happy that he started to sing. He was so involved in his tune that he forgot to think. He sighed an enormous sigh and, just as he gave up hope of ever seeing a woodland of big willow trees again, he had a brilliant idea.

He would scelf back in time to when the men were chopping down the trees. The willow elf scelfed so quickly and so purposefully that he propelled himself into the past with a loud *pop*!

Previously, he had stepped into the future a couple of times and walked into the Long Ago... he counted on his fingers: three times. He wondered if that was why he could not see very well. Maybe, he was out of practice. He was never too keen to delve into the past because he always felt like he was walking on eggshells. He had to be ever so careful not to do anything that could change the natural course of events. Maybe, he had scelfed so quickly that some of his elf-self had splintered off somewhere else because everything was so *bright*. His eyes watered as he squinted into the air that the willow canopy once occupied. How he wished it were night-time. Things were more obvious to him there. He never had any difficulty seeing in the dark.

The willow elf squeezed his eyes tight and tried to look into the light. It was no good; he simply could not see anything. All of a sudden, he could feel something smiling at him, and it made him gasp. He was not used to things smiling at him, at least not properly, in the sort of way that made his tummy flutter. He tried to open his eyes again but closed them because of the shining light. He did not like daylight.

He stilled himself and decided to look, but this time, he looked with his eyes shut. He could see loads of men hard at work chopping down the trees and cutting up the branches into thin strips. He felt fury rise in huge bubbles out of his mouth. Just as he was about to explode with rage in a true elfish style, he felt himself being swept up and lifted out of harm. His eyes burst open; the light flooded in. It hurt. He squeezed his tears out and rubbed his eyes. Again, he felt something smile at him as it held on to him. *The thing is sun-like*, thought the elf.

This was all too weird, decided the elf, for he knew the thing that was smiling at him was also protecting him from becoming upset. The thing dazzled him and, once the willow elf had calmed down, it placed him carefully on the ground.

Keeping his eyes closed, he looked into the woods, using all of his other senses, for this was turning out to be the strangest of encounters. This time, it was not as bright as when he had looked with his eyes open, but he identified an area in the woods that distinctively shone and sparkled. Curious, the elf looked steadily into the light. It was nothing more than a big clump of light. As he felt the true warmth of that smile again, the light radiated iridescent beams of silver and gold that mingled and jigged a celebratory dance of otherworldly magic.

The faery did not speak to the elf; it simply shone in a foreign manner that quite tickled him.

The willow elf felt lovely on the inside. He had never seen anything so enormous and interesting. This, he realised, must be what the little sprites called a faery. The willow elf did not know what to do because he had never been in the presence of such an enormous being. How powerful their sparkling magic must be and how different to an elf's. There must be all walks of life on the earth that he had never met. The faery's light rippled to a pearlescent shimmer, as if it was made of rainbows.

The elf wondered how they could live in so much light, but he felt oddly calm in the presence of the faery. In his mind's eye, he saw men standing in a row with enormous bows made from yew. They were practising shooting arrows.

The willow elf had a feeling that it was time for him to leave. He did not know how to speak the language of faery, but he wanted to say thank you, because without the faery's protection, he would have gotten so angry he would have exploded and expired. This faery had saved his life.

The only thing he knew that came close to the brightness of the faery was the light of the full moon, but he could not magic a moon. The willow elf closed his eyes and dreamed of saying thank you. As he did, a tiny orb of white light appeared by his ribs and flew ever so softly towards the faery, who caught it and rolled it around in his hands. The faery carefully wrapped fingers of light around it and, with that, disappeared into the daylight.

Not knowing quite what to do with himself, the willow elf scelfed back to the present.

It was early morning and a low mist gathered as warm steam rose out of the earth to meet the cold air. In his clearing, the willow elf thought about the faery. In his mind, there was no doubt that the faery was stunning, but the glum was where he felt comfortable. It was where he belonged. This was where he was most content.

Four little lights slowly approached the willow elf and floated like will-o'-the-wisps to the large willow tree. The willow elf looked up from his tree stump and smiled. *They're such nosey little people*, he thought to himself. A little gong bonged in the clouds of steam.

Upon hearing the elf thinking, the air sprites floated slowly closer because they did not want the elf to tell them to go away.

"Well?" asked Pizz.

"So?" enquired Whuz.

"Any news?" questioned Puzz.

"Anything?" ventured Whiz.

The willow elf relayed the tale of what had happened, of the faery who had protected him and all the elves from seeing what had happened. The faery had known, once the willow elves realised there was nothing they could do to change the world in which they found themselves, they would expire from weeping in the mud or explode like a fermenting brew. The willow elf explained to them that it was never a good thing for an elf to become too annoyed because when they start fizzing and heating up, they die. The faery had saved his life by preventing him from vaporising.

"Ooooo… lovely," exclaimed Puzz, flying up to a branch and thinking about the faery.

"What was that special light that travelled from your heart to the faery?" asked Puzz, flying back to the willow elf.

"A gift," said the willow elf.

Puzz looked at where her ribs would be and rubbed the area. Whuz, Whiz and Pizz tried it too but alas, nothing happened. Whuz flew around in tiny circles. Whiz sat on the elf's shoulder but stilled his wings so that he did not buzz, and Pizz rested on a leaf. The sprites were quiet for a brief moment and then flew off in different directions.

Gongs sounded quietly in the mist.

9

In a Little Room
Confining Mighty Men

The willow elf awoke at sunset. He scelfed back to the dark
woods to meet the red elf but could not find him. He decided
to think about what he needed to tell him because he knew
that his thinking would be heard far and wide by fellows with
similar sound receptors.

Stepping out of a yew hedge, the red elf held up his staff
and snorted.

The willow elf explained how he had seen another willow
elf working elf magic and that he was going to ask him if they

could work together. Then he asked the red elf if he wanted to join them because he had seen the King's men with yew bows and arrows. The red elf was surprised by his tale. However, he said he would come along in case the willow elf needed help but that he would not enter into the human den because yew tree elf magic could be dangerous to human beings.

When it was time to go, the willow elf turned to the red elf, who sucked in his cheeks in a very serious manner and nodded. Once they had scelfed into the woods near Owain's dwelling, the red elf chose to remain in the long grass near the cottage. The willow elf skipped off, hoping to meet the little elf. He looked up at the sky. It was a moonless night, and the stars brightened the dark sky like crystals sewn onto velvet.

Hidden behind the clay storage pots, the willow elf waited for the little elf to scelf back into Owain's cottage. He had decided that it was time to confront him. He had seen the little elf in the human den a few times, and he knew he was bound to turn up soon.

An owl screeched as it flew past the cottage and, with that ear-piercing sound, the little elf appeared on top of the woollen blankets and sheepskins that covered the human beings. When he was comfortable on the blankets, the elf brought out his wand and started to sing. On hearing a new sphere of gongs, the willow elf leaped out from his hiding place, bounded across the room and grabbed the little elf off the bed. He held him tight so that he could not scelf and pulled him up to his hiding place behind the pots and jars.

The little elf looked quite annoyed and pointed his wand at the willow elf. The willow elf thought that he was going to get quite an earful from the little elf and so, just as he thought that he was about to fizz with rage, he held up his finger and shushed him. Whereupon, the little elf looked outraged.

"Don't wake them," said the willow elf, pointing at the sleeping people.

The little elf looked shocked and pointed his wand at the willow elf.

"Wait! I need to ask you something," the willow elf said.

The little elf lowered his wand.

"Please can we work together?" said the willow elf, feeling like he was finally walking his walk and talking his talk.

The little elf's eyes widened and he nodded.

Three elves sat down in the long grass under the stars and an owl overheard the subtle sound of gongs playing in the night air. As they began to discuss what each one knew, the willow elf felt greatly troubled, for he had told the red elf about the yew bows. The red elf informed the others that he was going for a walk, but when he did not return and the atmosphere became silent, the willow elf began to sing about yew trees.

"Oh! Tree of poisonous berries not liked by sheep and cows. Oh! Tree of poisonous berries now big, heavy bows."

A large red ball rumbled towards him and the red elf jumped up, giving the little elf quite a fright.

"That's enough of that infernal racket," grumbled the red elf as he uncurled from his orb.

"We are going to scelf to see the King," said the little elf.

"Are we?" asked the willow elf.

"What on earth would you want to do that for?" said the

red elf to the little elf. "Have thou been meddling further? It's never a good idea to get involved with human affairs." He glared at him with his accusation.

The little elf started to chew his fingernails and the willow elf told him what they had seen and overheard: that the red elf's yew wood was to be made into bows. The willow elf said he thought that the willow shafts were to be arrows for the English archers, but he was not sure.

"I will find out for myself what has happened to *my* yew, but first I shalt go back to my dark woods, for I've had enough of all this gallivanting," said the red elf. He turned on his heels and walked off.

"Take a hike, then," said the little elf under his breath.

The willow elf gasped. How foolish he was to risk angering the yew elf. The willow elf grabbed his ear, for it was the closest thing to him, and they scelfed as quickly as they could.

The elves found themselves in a beautiful woodland with large oak trees and hazel. The willow elf plodded on. After a short while, he realised that he was on his own. He stopped, looked to the left and looked to the right, but the little elf was nowhere to be seen. He turned around and saw him standing at the edge of the woodland. The little elf stood with one hand on his hip and beckoned to him to follow. He walked back to meet him. The willow elf realised that he must have been walking in the wrong direction. As he approached, the little elf rolled his eyes up, turned around and walked off.

After he had followed for a while, the willow elf started to think that this little elf was different to other elves he had met. He was smaller, slightly light-footed and he felt softer, somehow. It struck him suddenly that this little willow elf was a she! He stopped in his tracks and stared after the little elf. How could he have been so slow to realise that he was a she? However, the little elf was quick to sense that something was afoot and she slowed. She turned around and wandered up to the willow elf. He continued to stare dumbfounded back at her. One side of her mouth curled upwards as she read his thoughts.

What a funny elf he is, she thought.

Once the elf recovered from his shock, he found his predicament quite funny and they laughed together. Every elf could be a bit silly and he could be very silly. He admitted to himself that, although it was unlike an elf to enjoy company, he was very much enjoying not being alone for the first time in his long, long life. As they walked, the willow elf and the little elf sang together, because that is what elves do best. She suggested to him that it was about time that they scelfed.

"I want you to see Henry the Fifth! There is also another man, a magical man. He'll like you."

The little elf sang to him of a battle that was going to happen where many men were going to fight and many more were going to expire.

The little elf had clearly been privy to these meetings before. She jumped from one of the high-backed chairs and sat on the edge of the oak table. The willow elf gazed around the room. In the middle of the table, there was a large vessel, from which the men poured a liquid into their goblets. The little elf told the willow elf that this was a drink made from hops. It was known as ale. The men were all dressed in fancy clothes, and the ale sprayed from their mouths when they spoke. The willow elf stared at the King, for he had never seen a King before. He had dark hair and, other than a deep scar on his face, he looked the same as all the other men. Then, the willow elf looked over to the little elf who was near to the King, with her legs dangling over the edge of the table, looking bored. She started to pick at her long, pointy fingernails.

Yuch, thought the willow elf, looking away.

The men discussed the intended battle, the number of men needed, weapons that they would use and strategies, until they had drunk quite a few goblets of ale. Then, they talked at the same time and never really listened to what the other had to say.

The willow elf looked back at the little elf and saw with horror that she was now chewing her long, dirty toenails with her brown, sharp teeth. The willow elf shuddered. As he did so, one of his knees jerked up so high that it hit him on his chin. The little elf stopped biting and picking and stared at him. *The willow elf looks like he's having a fit of the collywobbles,* the little elf thought. The willow elf moved away from the table and positioned himself in the room where he could not see his fellow conspirator.

As he surveyed his band of brothers in the room, the King felt confidence rise in his chest. *These men are made of solid stuff,* he thought. The meeting had gone on for hours, with the Great Council disagreeing to sanction war with

France, but now that he was in his private hall with his closest advisors, he knew that the real decisions would be made at his table. *Ale can make a man trust anyone or suspect a friend*, he thought to himself. These were mighty men, but did they have the courage to suggest a better plan than his own? Just then, he saw a Welsh nobleman, called Dafydd Gam, wink into the air as though he thought, or imagined to himself, that there was someone else in the room.

"Have you taken leave of your senses, man?" roared the King.

"Your Majesty, haven't we all?" replied Dafydd Gam, for the Great Council had been long, with noblemen insisting on negotiations with the French and politicians who were difficult to persuade.

The King did not like that statement. He did not answer. All heads in the room were turning between the King and Dafydd Gam. The King pushed out his chair and rose to his feet, whereupon the willow elf saw how tall he stood above the others.

"Explain your meaning, Davy Gam." The King addressed the Welsh nobleman by his informal title.

Davy Gam bowed his head courteously and then relaxed back into his chair. His wonky eyes sparkled as though he had a wonderful idea.

"Your Majesty, comrades. We will be outnumbered and even with the good grace of our Lord and your blessed presence, Your Majesty, the men will be tired from walking, hungry and ill from travelling, thus not energetically prepared for hand-to-hand fighting."

The King nodded for his esquire to continue.

Davy Gam looked back to the side of the room where he

had previously winked into the air. An astonished willow elf stood as still as a gargoyle and stared back at the Welshman with golden hair.

Then, Davy Gam addressed the King, "Thank you, Your Majesty. I mean that, rather than foot soldiers, we should use archers and the Welsh longbow made from Welsh yew."

There were a few guffaws round the table. Davy Gam put his elbows on the table and levelled them in the eye.

"For it is the Welsh longbow not an English longbow. We can use every commoner who has practised archery, every able-bodied man in our realm, poor and rich alike, who have used archery at games and in holidays. For men will never shoot well unless they were once boys brought up with bows and arrows and have a strong left arm."

There were fewer remarks this time and the nobleman was undeterred. He looked directly at the willow elf, smiled and dipped his head in respect of the immensely wise creature in the room. Despite their attempt to ridicule Davy Gam, there could be no disputing that archery was by far their best option, and so the mighty men said no more.

The King noticed a change of atmosphere as all pairs of eyes in the room were rooted back on him.

"So, it shall be. The *Welsh* longbow, made from a single piece of wych elm or yew. But it will be known as the war bow. The waxed strings will be made of hemp. The men will spend the eve of battle in silence," said the King. He stood up and downed the contents of his goblet.

The men raised their goblets into the air, cheered and finished their ale, too.

The King continued, "My foresters will be sent out to look for trees. The arrows will be made of poplar, hazel, ash and beech, with goose feathers. My blacksmiths will make the heads. The bows will be collected in the counties and all stored in the tower. The men-at-arms will be lightly armoured; the English and Welsh archers will form most of my army."

Davy Gam turned to the willow elves and, pretending to admire the fine carving on the surface of his chair, he raised his goblet to salute his invisible friends. As he lowered his head in honour, the King mistook it for a modest courtesy.

When the men were talking together, Davy Gam stood up and walked up and down the hall to stretch his legs.

"Elf, I have a great favour to ask of you. Can you place magic in the arrows to make them fly high and fast?" he asked quietly.

The Welsh nobleman was shorter than the King and possessed a kindness in his eyes. Tapping at his forehead to indicate that he would think about it, the willow elf held on to the little elf's arm, and together they scelfed back to his clearing.

10

Unleash the Scunner

Tonight, many sad-sounding gongs rang in the clearing where the tree stumps lay. The willow elf pondered something terrible. What if he was responsible for the demise of the willow trees, yew trees and other trees? If Davy Gam had not spied him in the room, perhaps he would not have had such a grand idea. The thought was terribly unsettling. If it was the truth, the willow elf knew that it was him and him alone who would have to put it right. However, in the same jangle of gongs, he thought it was the little elf who had taken him there in the first place. Why had the Welsh nobleman not asked her to help him with magic? Could the nobleman not see her? The nobleman was highly unusual. In the Long Ago, humans had the ability to feel and sense elves, but other than Owain's baby, he had never heard of people who could actually see elves. It was not in any elf lore.

We should never have scelfed back in time, he thought. Gongs sounded by the river as if they were all crashing into each other. The willow elf was worried, for there was no guarantee that Owain's willow saplings would grow into big trees. He thought about the stream that ran near to Owain's cottage, which fed the river near his tree stumps. At least the saplings will have enough water.

There was another problem, for when he walked outside the perimeter of what was once his patch of willow trees, he always mysteriously found himself back in his old home by a familiar tree stump. The tree stump was the one that he was sitting on when it occurred to him that something was greatly amiss. For some time now, wherever he fell asleep, he woke up back on his tree stump. That meant there was another mystery in his wood.

All of a sudden, the willow elf fell backwards, as if unseen arms had swept him off his feet and, once more, he floated off horizontally and backwards up into the Spiral Earth Tone. He floated as if seated on an invisible chair whilst the other elves fought with their arms and legs for balance. He allowed himself to feel a little smug. Once all the elves arrived in the Spiral Earth Tone, they hung like Christmas decorations, blinking and swaying in the air. The willow elf saw the little elf hanging sideways and chewing her nails.

The guttural gong of the willow Ancients speaking in unison sounded with urgency.

"Unleash the Scunner!"

The willow elf gulped. He could feel a hot sensation spread from his neck, across his cheeks and into his ears. One by one, the elves turned and stared at him. He glowed quite a red. All the willow elves wondered what he'd been up to, but before they had time to make too much noise with all their thinking, the Spiral Earth Tone sent them home.

Back in his woodland clearing, the willow elf felt confused and grumpy. The Ancients had made him feel that he had been very naughty, but he still thought he had done the right thing. The Scunner had deserved it. She was not a very nice person, shape-shifter, animal thingy. Everyone knew that.

The willow elf sulked. He did not like being told to do things, especially things he did not want to do. He would have to go and find her and release her from his spell. It was not going to be something he enjoyed. He stomped his feet in the sawdust. She had not even helped him. However, he felt determined. He would find the help that he needed to get his trees back and maybe, if he looked in the right place, help would be found. He would go back to contact the Genius Loci, but first he had to face a very angry shape-shifter.

The willow elf scelfed.

He arrived at the same stream, with its rockpools and gnarled roots from ancient hawthorn and whitethorn trees. The moon was not shining tonight, and the water sprites were not playing. He carefully stepped over the large stones and stood looking at the boulder that the Scunner had squelched out from the last time he had visited her. He remembered that he had left her in the form of a woman. He raised his eyes up from the ground and gazed around the landscape. Humans live in dwellings. She could be anywhere by now.

Realising that he would have to magic her to his side, he imagined what she might be doing at this moment. He remembered her washing her feet and hands in the stream and playing with her long, dark hair. Then, the willow elf heard singing. He followed the sound and found the Scunner eating berries. Her hands were stained yellow, red and purple from the juice of the fruit.

"Poisonous, these ones, but they can't hurt me. You really are a noisy elf. What is that gaggle of gongs and singing I can hear? Is that *really* you?"

The willow elf nodded.

She turned her nose up in disgust and said, "Come on, then. Get on with it."

The willow elf did not know *how* she knew what he was there to do, but it did not matter, for he had received his orders to release her. He stood some distance away, ready to scelf, in case she shape-shifted into a huge lion or a dragon. He looked into her eyes. This time, she levelled her eyes with his and spoke to him.

"Elf, I like this form. It's interesting being a human being. Simple but fascinating."

The willow elf was surprised by her words, but she was not going to trick him. He sent his magic hurtling through the air towards her. She fell over backwards from her boulder.

The willow elf watched as she played with various physical forms. She was checking that she had all of her magic back. Finally, she chose the form of an elf and stood facing him.

This unnerved the willow elf. He moved further away. She took a big step towards him. He took a big step back. She took a few more steps towards him and, cautiously, he took another few steps back. Then, she stopped and smiled at him.

"After you forced me into one form, I learned many new things. Thank you."

She took a small step closer. The willow elf stood his ground. He wondered if this time, she might help him.

"The King does not want your willow for his arrows. He wants the willow to take in his baggage train for healing purposes and to make into baskets."

A sphere of gongs resonated in the air as he thought about what she had said.

The Scunner changed back into human form.

"Willow Elf, sometimes we search too far for answers, when the truth can be found nearer to home."

11

Revisiting the Genius Loci

The Scunner had said that answers were nearer to home. The elf wondered what this could mean. He was not going to contact the sprites because they would fill his head with chatter. He would speak to the Genius Loci.

"Genius Loci, helloooooo," sung the willow elf.

He sat still for a while. Nothing happened. He decided to try a different approach.

"Genius Loci, essence of this woodland and of our home, I call to theeeee… I am one of many willow elves."

Still, nothing happened.

"Hear my call of walking and singing, of singing and

walking."

That sounded better.

"Arise, erm, rise, Genius Loci."

He desperately needed inspiration. He decided to lie on the ground on his belly and rub his face in the soil, not because he was sad but because he thought that it might bring him closer to the Genius Loci. It worked.

He looked around himself. Nothing looked different, but something felt different. It was as though an atmosphere in the woods had become more tangible. The willow elf felt nervous and excited all at the same time. He jumped up and down with joy and then felt very silly because he knew he was not alone; the Genius Loci watched him.

"I do not judge you, Willow Elf."

The willow elf roamed the leaves and wilderness for the source of the sound. He could not see anything different around him, and he scoured the vegetation. Round and round, he looked for the Genius Loci.

"You are wonderful," said a voice in the clearing. "Just like all of the earth's beautiful creatures. Thank you for calling. Have a wonderful day. Goodbye."

"No! Don't go away!"

"You need something, I know, but I do not 'gift' things," said the Genius Loci.

"But I need to access magic. What am I missing this time? What do I not see? What do I now know?"

"Nothing! I know you have met the man who will help you, but growing trees takes time. In the earth are seeds that have heard your call. They are busy meditating upon their cellular magic. You will have willow trees, but you have to be patient. Nature knows best. I am happy now. Thank you, Great Elf."

"How did you know that?"

"Ah! Well, the Green Lady told me," whispered the Genius Loci.

"Who's that?" said the willow elf, feeling baffled.

"She lives in the ancient willow tree, but she has not been here as long as me. Davy Gam asked you to put magic into the arrows so that they fly fast. Is this true, Great Elf?"

The willow elf looked at his toes, for it was true, but he had not agreed to do it.

"The Green Lady told me that in order for that to happen, you must ask the permission of the Willow Dryad."

"Oh! Dear me."

The willow elf had not realised that. It would not be easy to ask one of the oldest spirits on the earth for help.

12

The Green Lady

The willow elf was confused. Why did the King want to be the monarch of another place when he was already King of this island? It made no sense to the willow elf, who knew that the land belonged to otherworldly creatures as well as animals and human beings. It struck him as even odder that he had a role to play in all that was unfolding. Elves knew their limitations, and the willow elf knew he could not prevent many men from dying on an unknown battlefield. Surely, it was a strange power that a king possessed if he could determine the lives and deaths of so many of his kinsmen. The willow elf decided that on the day of the battle, he would not scelf to the land across the sea. For it was not practical to have an elf present. In truth, he did not want to see what would happen on that day. He was sure that the elves and all other magical creatures would conceal themselves in trees, scelf off somewhere quiet, or disappear further into another world, underworld, or upperworld, until the men had stopped hurting each other.

The King had decided that his archers would use the Welsh longbow. Davy Gam had a grand plan: he would get the willow elves to magic all the arrows to fly swiftly. The willow elf needed the cooperation of the Dryad. However, seeking the help of the Willow Dryad, and asking for his help, terrified him. The earth was the Dryad's domain. Surely, he didn't understand the ways of men. If the Dryad didn't agree to help, he was sure the elf Ancients would not entertain the nobleman's request.

The only thing he did know for certain was that when the little elf wasn't walking with him, she was close to Owain making sure he planted more trees. The willow elf sat down on a tree stump and spoke to the Genius Loci. He assumed he was here somewhere, even if he could not see him.

"How do I meet the Green Lady of the great willow tree?" he asked.

"I will call upon her," replied the Genius Loci immediately. "Go and look for something to give to her. She'll like that."

After a few moments, the willow elf heard a great whisper whirl in the air as the atmosphere tingled with magic and the plants shimmered, as if the world around him was made of a fluid.

"She is on her way," came the words from the Genius Loci.

The little elf held up her wand in caution and the willow elf watched, fascinated, as the great willow tree moved closer to him, as if it were a hologram. The willow elf looked to see if the tree had grown feet, but he could not see any. His eyes brightened as a woman stepped out of the trunk.

The Green Lady was as tall as the tree, with green skin and long green hair. She walked all the way around the trunk of the tree before looking at the willow elf.

Deciding that he ought to oversee the occasion, the Genius Loci introduced the willow elf to the Green Lady.

"The Green Lady," he announced in a serious tone. He was enjoying his new role as a master of ceremonies.

"Nice to meet you. I am a willow elf."

The Green Lady smiled. "It is a pleasure to meet you too, Wise Elf, but I have met you many times." She was not spirit-like at all but quite solid-looking and in a fine embroidered dress.

"Oh? I didn't know you existed. Why is it that I have never seen you?"

"Willow Elf, you can't see properly in daylight. Many things escape your sight. You see in the glum. Every day you sleep in the willow trees, and when the sky suggests it is getting dark, out you come."

"Ah!" The willow elf nodded.

"And when the sun is thinking about rising, you ready yourself to go home and back into the trees," she continued.

The sprites had been listening in and they suddenly started talking.

"We know he sleeps in the daytime," said Whiz.

"What did you do in *your* tree, Willow Elf?" said Puzz.

"I slept."

Then, the willow elf thought to himself that although the Green Lady lives in the tree, she was not the tree's keeper. Everyone heard the little gongs bonging together. Puzz looked around, determined to catch a glimpse of a gong one day.

"You are a humble being, Willow Elf, and very powerful. Perhaps, it is best that you do not know how powerful you are. Willow trees are the trees of dreaming. Willow elves can make magical things happen through dreaming and they do not fear responsibility." The Green Lady addressed the tiny audience. "And I have watched this willow elf for a long time but mostly when he was sleeping."

"Are there a lot of Green Ladies?" asked the little elf.

"Yes. There are many. And when my trunk withers, I shall jump into another tree, but that takes a lot of preparation, and I hope it doesn't happen for a long, long time."

Remembering that he had carefully selected some lovely leaves, twigs and a pebble, the willow elf laid his offerings at the trunk of the great willow tree.

"Thank you, Willow Elf. I have a confession to make."

"Huh?" said the willow elf, feeling that life was far too complicated.

"The faery who swept you up when the men were cutting

down the willow trees kept you safe for a while, but when he placed you down on a tree stump, you were quite confused. I took you in," she said.

"In where?" he asked.

"Into the great willow. Every morning when you fall asleep, I bring you to my home so that you can sleep peacefully. There is a lot of space in the great willow, you know. I could keep ten elves in there," she laughed.

The willow elf realised there was much he did not know and that there were many magical creatures looking out for each other. He had not seen the men in his part of the woodland because the faery had intervened. With the Green Lady housing him every night to protect his dreaming – so that he did not magic anything terrible out of disappointment or fear – he had been living in a sort of protective bubble.

"In the morning, I place you on your tree stump," she said.

"Green Lady, you are kind. Thank you," he said.

Silenced by the news, the sprites had not whizzed or pizzed in some time. The willow elf looked at them and laughed. *They're funny little things*, he thought.

Then, the willow elf suddenly remembered what he was meant to be doing.

"I am going walking soon. To find the Willow Dryad to ask for his help. A Welsh nobleman has asked for magic to be stowed in the arrows for the King's archers. I haven't promised the nobleman because I have never met the Dryad and he might not be that friendly. But, without his authority the magic won't work."

The Green Lady looked very serious.

"Yes, I know, Elf. That is why I present myself, for you cannot approach the Dryad. You do not know his realm and it is unlikely he will grant you this request."

The willow elf sat down on the sawdust, looking deflated, and the sound of gongs clattered in the air like a garden wind chime in a storm.

"I will ask for you," said the Green Lady, smoothing her verdant, long hair.

The sprites suddenly buzzed around the willow elf, and he felt a spring in his knees.

"Can you?" he asked.

"Wait here," she said and stepped into the wide girth of the monumental willow tree.

The Green Lady stepped out of the other side of the tree and into another world exactly like the one where the otherworldly creatures waited. Her long, green robes swished around her feet as she moved through the tree stumps. She stopped, held her hands out, closed her eyes and waited.

A stillness fell in the land and all the earth's creatures stopped what they were doing: the ants stopped foraging; the fox stood still; and the birds landed on the closest branch and waited. It was not long before a small, brown, cloaked and hooded figure, holding a wooden staff, appeared in the distance.

The Green Lady opened her eyes. It was a long time ago when a green lady had last asked the Dryad to help in the goings-on of humans. She could walk no further because she was at the maximum distance from the tree. If she took another step, she would sever her connection. Slowly, the Dryad floated towards her.

"Thank you for coming, Father Dryad. How is your Lady?"

The Dryad nodded his head once.

"I am here with a strange request from one of the earth's consorts: a willow elf."

The Dryad nodded again for her to continue.

"The human King of this land wishes war in a foreign land. His nobleman asked for their arrows to be blessed with speed and agility."

"Why would I grant this request?" the Dryad asked in a deep whisper.

"'Tis a good question," she replied and walked in a little circle to prepare what she wanted to say. "It is known amongst the Green Ladies that the Welsh nobleman is from an ancient family of Druids. You are familiar with their ways, Father Dryad. You know that they respect the land, plants and all of nature's hidden bounties, that they honour the sun and track the path of the moon. They hear nature's songs, creatures and the earth. This battle will happen and the Welsh nobleman who requested this magic will not return. The King will survive the battle; he will come home but he will not become the King of France. We will never understand the ways of mankind, for their ways are not our ways and they are increasingly not the old ways. However, if we keep an alliance with the Welsh nobleman, hopefully more of his kind will honour our ways and, in time, their children will walk the path of the wizard with magic; the way of the healer with intuition; the dance of the medicine man with his plant lore; and the jig of the sorceress with her knowledge of the elements. This is why I think you should honour his request, for this co-creation is rarely observed. The King already has other magic bestowed upon him, for he survived an arrow to the face at the age of sixteen when he was saved by a medicine man's healing power of bees' honey."

"And this is why you did not allow the elf to come? Because he does not know the domain of man?" he asked.

"Yes, Father Dryad. You are correct. And he doesn't know this realm," she answered.

The Dryad moved this way and that way as he floated on the surface of the earth before answering.

"I will not create magic to harm or kill a man. The arrowheads that men craft will do that damage alone. I could grant the means of great speed and agility but not death to the King's enemy, for that is not a great, nor worthy, form of magic. It is not what the Earth wants, only a power that men seek. Therefore, Green Lady, I cannot help. The willow elf will have to design his own magic if he wishes to help this man."

The Green Lady thanked him for allowing her to visit his realm. She turned and walked back into the trunk of the great willow.

When the Green Lady came back into the willow elf's clearing, she told the willow elf that the Dryad had refused to help. She drew a symbol into the air and told the willow elf that this magical symbol should be drawn over every sheaf of arrows to protect them from fire, but he would need to use his own magic to protect the arrows from the hands of thieves. The Green Lady also told the willow elf that he must never mention the Dryad to others because some things should always remain a secret.

13

Goodbye to Tree Stumps

The next night, the willow elf and the little elf walked together and thought long and hard about the elf Ancients until the Spiral Earth Tone whisked them up and backwards, into the air. In the elves' secret meeting place, they told the elf Ancients about the King's men, the proposed battle in France and the huge yew bows and arrows. They told the elf Ancients that they had obtained a magical symbol for a nobleman but not who had given it to them. The willow elf and the little elf told the elf Ancients that they had not put magic into the King's sheaf of arrows to give them speed and agility and that Davy Gam's men would have to do that for themselves.

After the willow elf had told the Welsh nobleman what magic he should use to prevent theft or fire, Davy Gam bent down to look at the willow elf. Crouched on one knee, he asked, "What is your name, my wise friend?"

The willow elf thought for a moment. It was a strange question to come from a human being. Elves' names remained hidden deep inside themselves because they harness magic. He looked carefully into each of the man's eyes. He saw no stranger there and no threat. He opened his mouth to say his name, but nothing came out. He closed it and opened it again, but the same thing happened. The elf decided that he must have forgotten his name entirely. Then, he realised he was not looking deep enough inside himself to collect the *shape* of his name. He looked harder, found his *name-shape*, and then he remembered.

"Hyk," he said.

"It is an honour to meet you, Hyk," said Davy Gam and repeated his words in Welsh. "*Mae'n anrhydedd i wybod eich.* May I call you Friend?" asked the Welsh nobleman.

The willow elf grinned a toothy grin.

"*Fy ffrind,*" said the Knight in Welsh. "We leave tomorrow for France."

After he had said goodbye to the nobleman, he scelfed into a part of the forest that was thick with hawthorn and holly. He padded around until he came upon the little elf, who was sitting on the ground blowing dandelion seeds into the air. He watched her for a while and slowly approached her.

"What's your name, little elf?"

Holding on to her dandelions, she looked at him. A chorus of gongs tinkled in the air.

"Brok," she said.

Hyk smiled his wonky smile and she smiled a toothy grin back. He could tell that they were going to be friends for a very, very long time. Together, they walked off to find Owain and to look after his willow trees, in case any pesky rabbits or deer fancied a midnight feast.

Many days after the battle of Agincourt, the little elf started to sing a merry tune and the willow elf thought that elves' thinking was just like their singing. It was tuneful. It was not baleful like the human's tunes about dreary, worldly woes. He had a funny thought.

"Am I getting wise?" chuckled the willow elf as he remembered the crazy elder elf.

The little elf shook her head and they both chuckled. Together, they scelfed to Hyk's willow clearing and shared a tree stump. The willow elf looked about him and realised that, for such on old creature, he was an impatient one. He had wanted the trees back immediately, but trees don't grow quickly; they grow slowly and elegantly from a seed. He stood up on his big feet and prowled the floor of the clearing for fresh green shoots and, sure enough, there they were – little trees were pushing up through the moss, leaves and what was left of the sawdust.

The willow elf wondered what had happened to all of King Henry's soldiers who died in battle. He wondered if they could all come back to life as little seeds because whilst elves expired and vanished into the atmosphere, humans did not – they were mortal. What, then, had happened to all of the French fighters? Were their bodies just lying out in the sun and the wind?

Sad gongs sounded in the air.

Brok looked at Hyk. She knew he felt bad.

"Don't trouble yourself with the worries of men, or you will start to think and live like one," she warned him. "Did you know that our Welsh nobleman saved the life of the King?"

The willow elf had not heard that tale and he thought of the nobleman, who had not returned.

"I want to scelf to the battlefield in France. Come with me," said Hyk.

The elves held hands and scelfed.

A low breeze caught Hyk's ears as he appeared at Agincourt and Brok gasped.

"Oh dear," she said.

Together, they stood on an embankment and stared at the site of the battle, for there were no real soldiers anywhere but hundreds of ghosts. They were all talking to each other, saying, "*Bonjour, bonsoir.* Hello, good evening. *Noswaith dda.*" Bore da!

"I thought they didn't like each other," said Hyk.

"No, I think that's just the kings and noblemen. These are just, just… *men*," replied Brok.

From their raised spot in the landscape, they could see

men blowing out little puffs of smoke into the air from pipes, playing on lutes, rebecs and fiddles.

"How long will they stay here for?" asked Hyk.

"I don't know, but we need to do something," she said.

"*Fy ffrind*," spoke a voice in Welsh.

Hyk turned and saw the ghost of Davy Gam. "We are waiting a long time for the battle to start," he said.

"I'll never get involved with men again," said Hyk. "I'm sorry, my friend. We must leave now. Goodbye, Davy Gam."

Back at the willow stumps, Brok said, "Ah-ha! I know. We should have a bun dance. To help the soldiers on their passage to the land of the great yew trees," she said.

"There is a land of great yew trees?" asked Hyk, realising that was another thing that he did not know.

"Oh, yes!" said Brok.

"Can we go there?" asked Hyk.

"*No!* Not until it is our time, and it isn't that time yet. We'll go there when it is our time to expire, but I don't even know when that'll be. We've been here so long," she said.

"What's a bun dance?" asked Hyk.

"I don't know. I just invented it, but I am sure we can dream up something and make some magic," she said excitedly. Then, as quickly as she had said it, she had an idea. She jumped up, dropped her dandelions and started running.

"Wait! Where are you going?"

"To see the Scunner," she shouted back at him and scelfed.

The next day, an odd group of creatures gathered around the enormous weeping willow tree. There were two willow elves, four sprites, one red elf, an elder elf with shiny bells on his ankles, a tall Green Lady, a brilliantly bright faery and a grotty-looking female known as the Scunner, holding a broom made from willow. The red elf glowered at the Scunner until she told him that they would need his magic for their ceremony, and the elder elf got such a fright when the Genius Loci spoke to him that he nearly jumped out of his waistcoat. Brok tried to snatch the broomstick from the Scunner when she wasn't looking, but the Scunner shrieked, "It's mine. Ayes made it," at which the little elf had to let go.

"I am sorry that I brought you the bad news of the bows," said the willow elf to the red elf.

"I know that, Hyk, but I had to find out for myself. I scelfed into the Tower of London."

"Stop jangling! It's time to start the game," instructed Brok, pointing her wand at the two elves. Then, she used her magic to dream up a huge pile of sweet brioche buns. "We're going to have a bun dance," she replied happily, waving her wand.

No one knew what a bun dance was, so everyone remained quiet. Only Puzz was curious and bold enough to enquire, "What's that, then?"

"Elf magic works like this: the more you give the more you have! We have one yew tree berry for every solider that did not come home to our land or go home in France. Every bun has lots of them." She held up a brioche and the fun began.

The Scunner decorated the bread with poisonous yew tree berries. Then, the willow elf dreamt of willow catkins and opened his hands to find them full of such catkins, which he pressed into the middle of every bun. Then, the red elf made the buns float in the air in red baubles of light.

"This is quite a creative happening," said the Genius Loci, sounding grand.

Puzz, Pizz, Whiz and Whiz fluttered around the faery. They watched the scunner scatter the red berries on the top of the brioche buns.

"All we have to do is throw the buns in the air, someone else bursts them and that's a handful of soldiers in the land of the great yew trees. How long the soldiers stay there for is their business. The magic doesn't work unless the bun is air-bound. Catch!"

Brok threw the first one to Hyk, who caught it and threw it back up into the air, whereupon the red elf surrounded it in a red bauble of light. Hyk waited for it to float down like a red bubble and smashed it with his hand. Bread and berries scattered in the air and fell to the ground. Then, Brok threw one to the red elf, who missed it but picked it up and headbutted it, whereupon it burst into colour.

At Agincourt, lots of groups of ghosts were suddenly vanishing.

"I can't go further than twenty paces from this tree so don't go far," said the Green Lady. "You will have to celebrate your bun dance here."

"We will not exclude you, fine Lady," said the elder tree elf, catching a bun in his hat. He put his hand in his hat, rummaged around and pulled out three buns, which he threw to her all at once. They bounced off her hands and burst into an array of green.

"One day, there will be an abundance of willow and yew in this part of the earth," exclaimed Brok, as she thrust a handful of buns at the Scunner.

The sprites lifted the buns with magic and blew them to each other. The red elf whacked the buns with his staff because he knew that, for every bun thrown, there were seeds that might grow into trees new yew tree. Never before had there been such a commotion in the clearing, and never before had there been so much fun. Only for a moment did the willow elf wonder what the elf Ancients would think, but a bun hit him on the head and he stopped thinking.

Lightning Source UK Ltd.
Milton Keynes UK
UKHW011243200622
404687UK00003B/864